Along the Santa Fe Trail

Penn Mullin

High Noon Books
Novato, California

Cover Design and Interior Illustrations: Michael Cincotta

International Standard Book Number: 1-57128-115-0

10 09 08 07 06 05 04 03 02 01
2 1 0 9 8 7 6 5 4

Contents

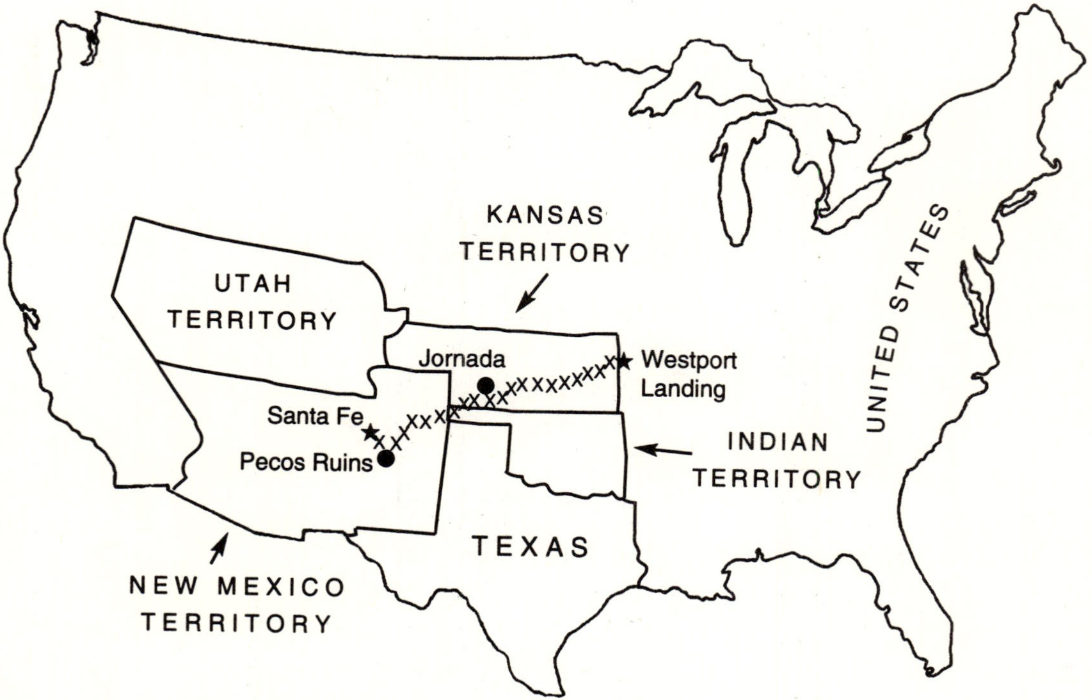

The Santa Fe Trail

CHAPTER 1

Packing Up

"This is a heavy load I've got," Pa told Liz. They stood by a big pile of wood crates. "My oxen can't pull it all the way to Santa Fe. Some of them will give out."

"What will you do then?" Liz asked.

"I will have to take more oxen. They can walk behind the wagon. Do you think you could keep them in line for me?" Pa asked.

Liz stared at Pa. Did he really ask her to go to Santa Fe? It was a long hard trail from here in Westport Landing, Missouri. Eight hundred miles! Pa drove his wagon south to Santa Fe each May. It was filled with things to trade to the Mexican people there. Her brother, Ned, got to go with Pa. He was fifteen, two years older. And now Pa wanted her to go, too!

"Sure! I could keep those oxen in line!" Liz said. "When do we leave, Pa?"

"Better check if Ma says it's OK," said Pa. "First help me pack up these tools and knives. Folks in Santa Fe will be sore if I don't bring them," Pa said.

Liz helped Pa load the crates. She packed up long rolls of cotton cloth and wool blankets. The Mexican people would trade Pa silver, gold, and furs for such things.

Then Liz ran to ask about the trip. Ma was rolling out a pie crust. Baby Meg played on the floor at her feet.

"Pa asked me to go to Santa Fe! I can help with the oxen. Can I go?" Liz asked.

Ma put down her rolling pin. "Santa Fe is a hard trip," she said. "The trail is not an easy place for a woman. There are big deserts to cross. There will be Indians. The hot sun beats down day after day. And it's hard work, Liz! Three months of it till you get back!"

"But *you* went once," Liz said.

Ma frowned. "Yes, once. But it was not easy. Our wagon sank in the river. Four of our oxen drowned."

"But I'll be OK. I really want to go, Ma. When I get home I'll help you."

Ma laughed. "You'll be too tired!"

"You mean I can go?"

"Yes, Liz. Pa needs your help on this trip," Ma said. "And I see how much you want to go. There will be bad days, though. You'll wish you had never left home. But you'll get to the end of the trail. And when you do, Liz, you'll feel so proud! I still think of that day when we first drove into Santa Fe!"

CHAPTER 2

"Roll 'Em"

This was leaving day! Pa's wagon sat in a huge field by the river. The field was filled with wagons like his. Their big white canvas tops snapped in the warm May wind. A large steamboat was docked at the river. This had brought people from states in the East.

Pa's twelve oxen were hitched up to the wagon. A big wooden yoke went around each pair's head. This helped Pa steer them. The air was filled with noise. Oxen bawled. Men yelled.

Whips cracked.

Pa and Ned were in the back of the wagon. Liz and Ma stood below with a list.

"Flour – 130 pounds!" Liz called out. "Bacon – 125 pounds! This is a lot of food!"

"You'll be hungry!" Pa said.

At last the list was done. Then Ma held up three pies. "Oh, thanks, Ma!" Ned laughed. "Pa never bakes on the trail!"

"Now, you just wait!" Liz said. "I make a good peach pie."

Then they heard the call, "Chain up!" Liz felt her heart pound. This was it. All of a sudden she felt scared.

"Time to go!" said Pa. He hugged Ma and Meg. "Liz, better go check your oxen."

"Now, be sure to wear your sun bonnet," Ma said. "I don't want to see you with freckles! Make sure Ned washes up at night. And take good care of Pa!"

Pa swung up into the wagon seat and picked up the reins. Ned got on his horse.

Liz hugged Ma one more time. Then she ran to her oxen. She heard the call, "Roll 'em!" and the wagons began to move. She turned to look for Ma and Meg. They stood by their small cart, waving in the dust. Soon Liz could see them no more.

CHAPTER 3

Good News

Liz sat by Pa on the wagon seat. Ned rode in back on his horse and watched the oxen. They had been on the trail for six hours. Liz looked out at the rolling prairie with its tall green grass. It seemed to stretch on and on like the sea. When the wind blew, the grass moved like waves.

There were twenty wagons in their train. They were spread out in rows of two or three on the wide trail. Liz looked into each one that went by. But she saw no other girls and very few women.

"Wait till we get to Council Grove," Pa said. "Then this wagon train will shape up. We choose a captain, and he makes you stay in lines. Then if there's trouble, you can corral the wagons fast."

"What kind of trouble?" asked Liz.

"Pawnees or Comanches might ride up. Most times they just want to trade. But not always," Pa said. "They are not happy to have us on their lands."

"How many trips to Santa Fe have you made, Pa?" Liz asked.

"I first came on the trail with my pa in

1828. He was a trader, just like me," Pa said. "That was 20 years ago. Back then we did not know where to cross the rivers. We got lost on the Jornada (Jor-NA-da). There were no wagon ruts to guide us."

"What's the Jornada?" Liz asked.

"The big desert. To cross it saves many days' time on the trail. In Spanish it means 'a journey,'" Pa told her. "There will be no water for 60 miles. A man named Becknell found this shortcut in 1822. His men almost died of thirst when they got lost on it."

Liz felt a chill go down her spine. "And we have to cross this same desert?"

"We'll be fine. I know it well by now," Pa

said. "I make sure to take *lots* of water!"

"Corral up! Corral up!" came the call. The wagons slowed down.

"Time to stop for the night," Pa said. "We'll all camp in a circle by that spring."

It felt good to get off the wagon. Liz did not know the ride would be so bumpy. They stopped in the cool shade of some trees. She helped Pa and Ned unyoke the oxen to graze and drink.

Ned came up beside her. "I'm sure hungry!" he said. "When do we eat, Liz?"

"Soon as you make a fire," she told him. "Ma packed us some stew." This first meal would be easy. From then on they would be on their own. She knew Pa and Ned were counting on her. But Ma had shown her how to make a few things. Liz got the cook box from the back of the wagon. It held all the things they'd need to cook with. Ma's stew was in the Dutch oven. This was a heavy iron pot with a lid. It had legs so it sat right down on the coals. Liz found a fry pan and a coffee pot. Ma had not forgot tin knives, forks, spoons, and cups.

Soon Ned had a fire lit. The air was filled with smoke from all the campfires. It feels cozy, Liz thought. She liked it inside the ring of wagons. If only she would see another girl here. The traders had just brought sons! Liz put the pot of stew on the coals to heat. She thought

Soon Ned had a fire lit.

about Ma. What was she doing now?

Just then she heard the sound of music! Who was playing a fiddle? She walked toward the sound. A tall man with red hair played the fiddle. Someone sat in the back of the wagon behind him. Liz got closer. Then she saw her – a girl her own age! She was wrapped in blankets. Her face was pale and tired.

Liz walked up close to her. "Hi! I'm Liz Blake from Missouri. I'm so glad I'm not the only girl!" she said.

"Pleased to meet you," the girl whispered. "I'm Pru Dodd. We're from Boonville. I came with my pa. He was scared to bring me because I've been sick. But my ma died. So I had to come with him."

How awful to lose your ma! "I'm so sorry," Liz said. "Are you better now?"

"Yes, I am," Pru said. "The fresh air is good for me. Will you come and see me again?"

"Oh, yes, I will!" Liz told her. "I'll come a lot. Do you like plum pie? I'll bring you some tonight!"

Liz ran back to her own fire to fix supper. The stew would be hot by now. And now she hummed a tune to herself. She had good news to tell!

CHAPTER 4

Crazy Weed!

It was dark. Liz felt someone shake her. "Wake up!" Pa said. Where am I? she thought. Then she knew. I'm in the wagon bed. But it's so dark. She crawled out from her quilts. The air was still cold. She could hear people starting fires. She pulled on her long dress and tied on her apron. Then she jumped down from the wagon. It was hard to see in the dark.

"I've made the fire," Liz heard Ned say. "You can cut some bacon. Pa went out to the oxen. They were restless last night. Might have been a wolf."

"Pawnees?" Liz asked.

"They're close by," Ned said.

Liz hoped none of her oxen were gone. She called them her "gals" now.

Soon Pa came up to the fire. "None gone! I was sure there would be. It's good to have the men on night watch out there!"

Liz washed up the plates at the spring. Then she tied her oxen to the wagon. Pa and Ned yoked up the front teams. Just then she heard the shout, "Roll 'em! Roll 'em!" It was time to go.

Just then Liz heard a loud rumbling sound.

It came up fast behind them. New wagons! Who were they?

Pa rode his horse up to the wagons to talk. Then he came to Liz. "They're off to Oregon. This is the cutoff. See, there they go!" They watched the long line of wagons turn off. "They have a long trail ahead. It will take 5 months. That makes our trail seem short!"

"Their wagons look small," Liz said.

"Next to ours, yes. Ours are built to haul all this heavy freight," Pa said.

"I think I'll go ride with Pru a bit," Liz told Pa. "If it's OK."

"Ned will watch your gals," Pa said.

Liz waved to Pru's pa, Jack Dodd, and

jumped aboard the Dodd wagon.

"Go on in! It will do her good to see you!" he smiled. "I know she gets lonesome."

Pru was propped up in a small bed. There were big boxes piled high all around her. Now her face lit up in a smile. "Liz! Where did you come from?"

"I just came in to say hi. How do you feel today?" Liz asked.

"All right. Just tired." Pru sighed. "The doctor said it would take a long time to get well. Maybe by Santa Fe!"

"Yes! You'll be well and we will dance in the Plaza! My pa told me what fun it is there," Liz said. "They have a big party when the wagons arrive."

"OK," laughed Pru. "We will dance in the Plaza! I promise you!"

Just then the wagon jumped. Then it lurched to the side. What was wrong?

"Pa!" screamed Pru.

Her pa yelled at his team and cracked his whip. The wagon shook and bounced. Liz felt her heart pound. The oxen had run wild! Pru's eyes were wide with fear.

All of a sudden a huge crate began to fall! It came towards Pru's bed. Liz knew she had to stop it. Fast. She threw herself towards the crate. It felt like a wall when she hit it. But she stopped it. The wagon shook and shook. Would it turn over? Just then it slowed down. Horses raced by. Liz held back more crates.

Then Pa jumped aboard. He hugged Liz and Pru tight. "You're safe! I was so scared you both might be hurt! There, the wagon's stopped now. The oxen ate crazy weed. It made them run wild."

Then Pru's pa, Jack, was there. His face was white with fear.

"Pa," said Pru. "Liz saved me! She kept that big crate from falling on me!"

"Liz!" said Pa. "That crate is big as you are! How did you do it?"

"Thank you, Liz! Thank you!" said Pru's pa. "I'm so glad you two are OK. I thought I'd packed things tight back there. I could not hold the team. Your pa's the one who rode up front and stopped them."

"I'm so glad I came to see you, Pru!" said Liz. "That was luck!"

"We have a plan to dance in the Plaza. Don't forget!" Pru told her.

"Oh, I won't!" Liz laughed.

"You and your pa will be guests of honor in camp tonight," Jack said. "You're heroes now and our new friends!"

CHAPTER 5

Buffalo!

The trail had changed now. The tall grass was gone and so were the trees. It was so flat you could see where the land met the sky all around.

Council Grove was behind them. There the men chose a wagon leader, Zeke Brown. He was a big, jolly man who laughed a lot. But he was a strong leader. Zeke said they should make fifteen miles a day. Santa Fe still lay 600 miles ahead.

Pa's oxen were strong. They pulled the big

load well. The hard part would be the Jornada, he said. Would they last 60 miles of hot desert? Liz took good care of her "gals." Pa showed her what crazy weed looked like. She would watch out for it on the trail so they would not eat it. "Babe" was the ox she liked best. She was fat and loved Liz to scratch her ears.

The days were long and hot. Liz rode with Pru when she could. Pru could sit up on the front seat now with her pa. Her face had a rosy glow. At night the two girls sat by the fire while Jack Dodd played his fiddle. Pru and Jack came for supper a lot. They loved the bread Liz baked in her Dutch oven. Ned and Pa said her beans were as good as Ma's. If Ned shot a sage hen, she made up a stew.

They had come more than 200 miles, Pa said. They were in the middle of the Kansas Territory. All they could see was a wide flat plain. It was buffalo range and Pawnee country.

One hot noon Liz heard a sound like thunder. But there were no clouds. The ground shook. Then she saw a huge line of dust far off. Men yelled and jumped on their horses. Buffalo! Liz froze. Would the herd come this way? She knew that buffalo will run right through a wagon train. Just then Pa rode up with his gun in hand. "I'll go get us one!" he yelled.

Liz sat with Ned and waited for Pa. They could see thousands of buffalo pass by. Now

They could see thousands of buffalo pass by.

and then they heard a gunshot. She wished Pa would come. What if he got trampled by the herd? At last all the men came back. They brought huge chunks of meat. Some rode back for more.

Liz would not forget the barbecue that night. People danced and sang at each fire. Pa showed Liz how he cooked the buffalo meat. Not one part was wasted. Some of the meat was smoked to use later on. She thought it tasted good. "But you have to chew it forever, don't you?" she asked Pru.

Liz fell asleep to the soft sounds of singing. Out on the prairie a wolf howled. But she felt safe, snug in her wagon bed.

CHAPTER 6

Names on the Rock

"Liz, look! It's Pawnee Rock!" Ned rode up to tell her. "We'll be there tonight! You have to climb it and carve your name. I'll go with you. We'll find my name!"

Liz looked where Ned pointed. She could see a small hill far in the distance. It was the only bump in the flatness of the plains. But it sure looked small.

All day they steered for the rock. Slowly it grew larger. Liz thought about what she would carve on Pawnee Rock.

All of a sudden she heard cheers and the thunder of horses. What was it? Pawnees? Then she saw it – a stagecoach! There were two men on top. One held a big rifle. A man waved from the window. And then it was gone. A shiny red blur.

"The stage is the fastest way to Santa Fe," Pa had told her. "Twenty-five days! But it's a rough ride. And it costs a *lot*!"

Liz stared after the stage. She wished she could have seen who was in it. Famous people? Ladies in fancy clothes? Why did it go by so fast?

They reached Pawnee Rock at the end of

the day. It was only 60 feet high. But it seemed like a mountain to Liz. She and Ned climbed it before supper. He found his name right away.

"I'll put mine next to it," Liz said. "Will you lend me your knife?" She carved in the rock: "Liz Blake and Pru Dodd. June 5, 1847." Then she sat back to look at her work. "A hundred years from now people will know we were here."

The sun was going down. There was a chill in the air. They could see the wagons pulled into a ring on the plain below. Campfires glowed in the dusk. Beyond them the land stretched wide and far into the night.

CHAPTER 7

The Jornada

The wagons were in their night circle. Campfires were lit. Liz set a pot of beans on to cook. She was so tired she ached all over. It had been a hard day crossing the Arkansas River. This was where Ma had lost her oxen on the trip with Pa. And Liz almost lost Babe. The river was not deep, but full of holes and quicksand. Babe went down and started to sink in the mud.

Then out of nowhere came a Comanche (Co-MAN-chee)! He threw a rope around Babe and pulled her free. Then he led her back to Liz. She gave him her mirror to thank him. And Pa had some bright green cloth for him. Soon the river was full of Comanches. They helped get wagons out of the mud and pulled oxen out of holes. The men paid them with tobacco and shirts. And then they were gone.

Now Liz felt better about Comanches. They had been friendly and kind. A proud, handsome people. She owed Babe's life to one of them.

Pa came up to the fire. "Look out there, Liz," Pa said. All she could see was an endless dry flat land. "There's the Jornada. The desert. We're in Mexican territory now. The next 60 miles will be rough. But we'll fill up with water here. Then we'll move at night to avoid the sun."

They rolled out on the Jornada at dusk the next day. They followed the deep wagon ruts carved in the sand. Liz walked with her "gals." Pa had now brought some of them up front. His oxen were tired. And the worst still lay ahead.

It felt strange to walk at night. The moon made the desert almost as light as day. Liz wished Pru could walk with her. But she was still much too weak.

Later Liz got in the wagon to sleep. Ned helped watch the "gals." Pa drove on through the night. Blazing heat woke Liz the next day. The wagons stopped. But there was no place to hide from the sun. No trees were in sight. The oxen lay down. Liz helped Pa and Ned water them. People got under their wagons to find shade. Liz had never felt heat like this. Her throat was so dry. She longed for night to come.

"Two of my oxen are sick," Pa said at supper. "They can't get up. This load was too much. We have to leave them."

"Leave them here? No!" said Liz. "They'll die. There are wolves all over!"

"I know, Liz. I'm sorry. But they can't walk. And we can't wait," Pa said. "I'll bring two of your oxen up front."

Just then Zeke, the wagon boss, called out, "Chain up!" It was time to go. Liz felt sad as she looked back at the two sick oxen left behind. What if one had been Babe?

They moved all night. Wolves howled in the distance. And the next day was the same. The sun blazed down. They ran low on water. The oxen drank so much. All of a sudden Liz called to Ned, "Look! There's a lake out there! See it?"

"No, Liz. It's not a lake. That's a *mirage* you see," Ned said. "It's a strange thing the light and heat do. It makes it look like a lake. A lot of folks die when they go out and try to find it. You see why they call this the Jornada del Muerto (MWER toe). Journey of Death."

"What an awful name," Liz said. "I wish

we were done with this place." But they still had two more days. She wished she could take off her long hot dress. Pa said there was a big spring at the end of this desert. Oh, to be there now!

Pru just lay on her bed in the wagon now. Liz put cold wet cloths on her head. She was worried about her friend. To dance in the Plaza seemed like a dream.

Two more of the lead oxen gave out. Now Babe had to go up front. The sick oxen had to be left. Liz cried as they rolled away from them. Now I know what Ma meant about the bad days, she thought.

It was the last night on the desert. The

wagons slowly set off.

All of a sudden they heard a low rumbling. Thunder! There was a cheer from all the wagons. And the rain came. People danced in it and filled their hats. Liz let the cool rain run over her face. Then lightning flashed. People got under their wagons or inside them. Then the tops leaked through. Near dawn the skies cleared. Zeke gave the order to go on. The end was near now. Spirits were high. Pa said the rain could save the sick oxen they'd left.

Soon they could see the green at the edge of the desert! "That's Lower Spring!" Pa said. "We're done with the Jornada!"

The wagons rolled into the grass now.

People got under their wagons to find shade.

There was the cool spring waiting. People dunked their whole heads into it. Oxen lined up to drink their fill. Then Liz saw Pru's pa lift her down from the wagon! Pru waved to Liz and began to walk towards the spring.

CHAPTER 8

The End of the Trail

They had been on the trail for 8 weeks now. And they were near Santa Fe at last. Rivers had been crossed, wagons mended. Now they were far south in the New Mexico territory. They could see snowcapped mountains ahead, the Sangre de Cristos (SAN-gray de CREE-stos).

"We take the pass through those. Then you can put on your best dress, Liz! We'll be in Santa Fe!" Pa told her.

"I can't wait! Pa, are there lots of dances in

the Plaza? Will there be folks there from the States?" Liz asked.

"Lots. The trail helped turn Santa Fe people towards the United States, away from Mexico. They wanted the good things we brought to trade. Now this territory belongs to us. General Kearney claimed it for us in 1846 in our war with Mexico. But not one drop of blood was shed when he took Santa Fe," Pa said.

Just then Ned rode up. "There's Pecos, Pa! Our last camp!"

There on the plains stood the ruins of Pecos – a huge church and city. Pa had told Liz about Pecos on the trail. It had been built by Indians hundreds of years ago. The thick walls of the church were 50 feet high. They were made of red adobe (a-DOUGH-bee) brick. The roof was now gone. The warm wind whistled through the high walls. And the wagons stopped in their shadow.

Liz could not sleep that night. All she could think of was Santa Fe. The wagons were off by dawn. They climbed through the pass. Santa Fe was soon before them. The town of red adobe houses had mountains all around. "There she is!" Pa shouted and threw his hat in the air. Liz felt her heart pound. They were here at last. All those weeks. The heat. The desert. She had made it just the way Ma said she would. And she did feel proud. She smoothed down the skirt of her dress. Pru waved from her wagon. She had ribbons in her hair. Ned wore his new red shirt. Pa had put on fresh clothes.

Babe was in the front pair of oxen now. She led them into Santa Fe. Liz was proud of her. They rolled into the narrow streets of the town. Crowds ran out to welcome them. "Los Americanos!" (Ah-mar-ee-CON-os) was the cry. They drove on to the Plaza in the center of town. Here in the big wide square the wagons stopped. Dust, noise, mules, traders, Indians, Mexicans – this was the Plaza. Liz stared at ladies who strolled in fancy clothes. She was glad she had saved a dress for today.

"Ned will help me unload," Pa said. "Liz,

you and Pru take a stroll. Here are a few coins to spend. Meet us back here in an hour. Then we'll go get supper. And you won't have to cook it!"

Liz and Pru walked around the Plaza. There was so much to see! Silver rings and bright turquoise beads were for sale. The air was filled with rich smells of spicy foods.

"Can you believe we're here?" Pru asked. "We said we would dance in the Plaza. But I never thought it would happen!"

"I know. I'd begun to think the trail had no end. But here we are! And you're well, too!" Liz laughed. "Wait! Do you hear music? It could be a dance. Let's go find it!"